THIS ONE 'N THAT ONE

in

YUM!

A Tale of Two Cookies

JANE SEYMOUR and **JAMES KEACH**

illustrated by
GEOFFREY PLANER

G. P. Putnam's Sons   New York

Library of Congress Cataloging-in-publication Data
Seymour, Jane. Yum! a tale of two cookies /
Jane Seymour and James Keach; illustrated by Geoffrey Planer.   p.   cm.
Summary: Although they are supposed to be in bed asleep, two kittens find a way
to join their parents, Lady Jane and Big Jim, for cookies on the beach.
[1. Cats—Fiction. 2. Parent and child—Fiction. 3. Cookies—Fiction.]
I. Keach, James. II. Planer, Geoffrey, ill. III. Title. IV. Series PZ7.S5235Th
1998   [E]—dc21   98-4787   CIP   AC   ISBN 0-399-23310-5
1 3 5 7 9 10 8 6 4 2
First Impression

Reprinted by arrangement with G.P. Putnam's Sons,
a division of Penguin Putnam Books for Young Readers.

To
Kris and John,
Kalen, Katie, Jenni, Sean, Thea, Erica,
Nina, Tom and Fizzy,
our inspirational friend Christopher Reeve,
and Jan of course!

And all the kids and all the kits around the world!

THIS ONE and **THAT ONE** were
getting ready for bed.
Lady Jane washed their whiskers.
Big Jim washed their paws.
Lady Jane washed their faces.
Big Jim washed their claws.

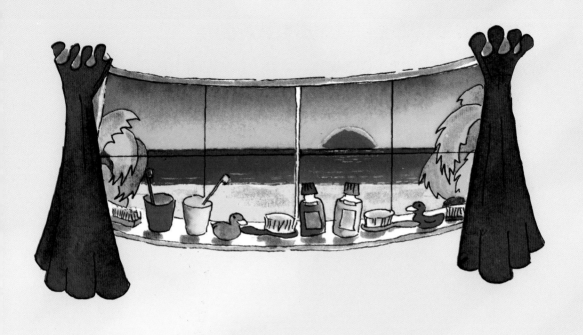

"What's that smell?" said **THIS ONE**.
"Just something cooking," said Lady Jane.

"What's that smell?" said **THAT ONE**.
"Just cookies," said Dad.

"COOKIES! CAN WE HAVE SOME?"
shouted **THIS ONE**.
"Not now. Those are Dad's fishing cookies,"
said Mom, trying to dry him.

"FISHING! CAN WE COME TOO?" said **THAT ONE**. "Not now," said Dad, trying to catch him.

Mom and Dad kissed the kits and
tucked them in.
"Yummy?" said **THIS ONE**.
"*Good night,*" said Mom.
"Tummy?" said **THAT ONE**.
"*Good night,*" said Dad.
"Cookies?" said **THIS ONE** and **THAT ONE**.
"Maybe tomorrow," said Mom and Dad together
as they went out of the room.

"I think the cookies will be too cold tomorrow,"
said **THAT ONE**.
"I think the cookies will be too old tomorrow,"
said **THIS ONE**.
"Those cookies will be gone tomorrow!"
said **THIS ONE** and **THAT ONE**.

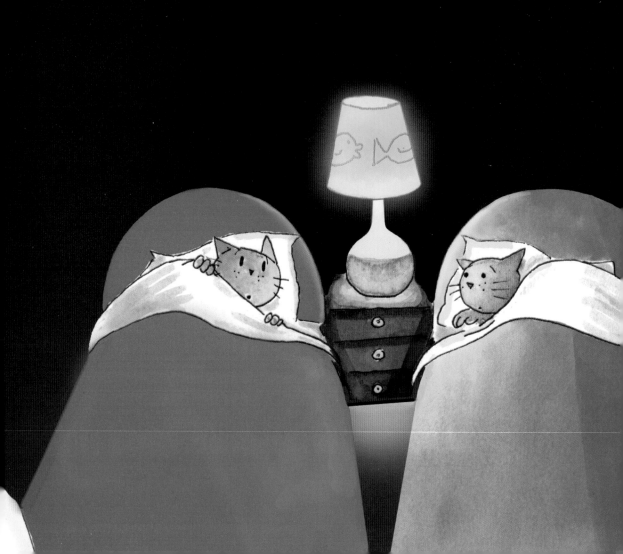

Downstairs in the kitchen,
Big Jim took a deep sniff.
"Mmmm . . . yummy. Are they ready?"
Mom looked at the cookies in the oven.
"Soon. I'll bring them out to you."

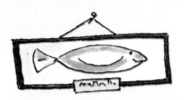

So Big Jim got his pole and his good luck hat
and headed down to the sea, singing,
"C'mon, fish, c'mon and bite—
you'd better be Jim's fish tonight!"

But up in their room, **THIS ONE** and **THAT ONE**
were not asleep; not a bit asleep.

"I can smell those cookies," said **THIS ONE**.
"I can see those cookies," said **THAT ONE**.
"I can taste those cookies!" said
THIS ONE and **THAT ONE**.

Lady Jane checked the cookies. They were just right. She wrapped them in a bag and put them into the old picnic basket.

Then she went off to brush up her whiskers and fluff out her fur before going out to see Big Jim.

Down the stairs slipped
two little kittens;

into the kitchen flew two little shadows;

up to the basket crept two little creatures.

"My, this basket has gotten heavy," said Lady Jane
as she dragged it down the sand to Jim.

Big Jim sat by the sea, looking sadly
up at the moon.
There were no fish, no fish at all.

Then he saw Lady Jane and he smiled.
"Cookies?" said Big Jim.
"Maybe," said Mom, and she snuggled up close
and started to purr a beautiful tune.

"Shall we dance?" she asked.

"Dance?!" said Big Jim.

"No dancing, no cookies!" said Lady Jane.

So Big Jim took Lady Jane's paw and they
danced on the sand by the sea.
Lady Jane looked deep into Big Jim's eyes.
Big Jim tried to look deep into the basket.

"It's time for cookies now, isn't it?" he panted.
"It is time for cookies now," said Lady Jane, laughing.

Big Jim took the bag from the basket.
He patted it. He shook it. He looked inside it.
NO COOKIES!

Then Big Jim looked inside the basket.
He saw two furry little heads!

THIS ONE jumped up!
THAT ONE jumped up, too!

They looked up and saw a very sad Dad.

"You ate all my cookies!" cried Big Jim.
"But I saved you a big one, Dad," said **THIS ONE**.
"And I saved you a big one too, Dad,"
said **THAT ONE**.
"And you ate thirty-four small ones,"
said Dad sadly.
"Oh well, it's better for your figure, Jim,"
said Lady Jane.
"But I've just done all that dancing," said Big Jim.

"DANCING? CAN WE DANCE TOO, DAD?"
shouted **THIS ONE** and **THAT ONE**.

THIS ONE looked at **THAT ONE**.
THAT ONE looked at **THIS ONE**.
Mom looked at Dad.
Dad looked at Mom.
"Save the last dance for me,"
Lady Jane said with a laugh.
"Save the last cookie for me,"
Big Jim said with a laugh.

11

"Shall we dance?"
And that is what all
four did.
Two fat little kittens and
Mom and Dad.
On the sand. By the sea.
By the light of the moon.

One paw here,
And one paw there;
High step, low step,
Up in the air.
Three paws, four paws
off the ground;
Dancing cats' paws,
'Round and 'Round.